TORN AWAKE

Also by Forrest Gander

POETRY BOOKS AND CHAPBOOKS

Rush to the Lake
Lynchburg
Eggplants and Lotus Root
Deeds of Utmost Kindness
Science & Steepleflower
The Hugeness of That Which is Missing

SELECTED TRANSLATIONS

Mouth to Mouth: Poems by Twelve Contemporary Mexican Women
Immanent Visitor: Selected Poems of Jaime Saenz (with Kent Johnson)
No Shelter: Selected Poems of Pura López Colomé
Of Their Ornate Eyes of Crystalline Sand: Poems of Coral Bracho

SELECTED TRANSLATIONS IN ANTHOLOGIES

The New Mexican Poets
The Oxford Anthology of Latin American Poetry
Poems for the Millennium: The University of California Press Book of Modern and
Postmodern Poetry/Volume II: From Postwar to Millennium
Light From a Nearby Window: Contemporary Mexican Poetry
Third Wave, The New Russian Poetry

FORREST GANDER

TORN AWAKE

A NEW DIRECTIONS BOOK

AUTHOR'S NOTE: My gratitude to Peter Cole and to Agha Shahid Ali and to George and Mary Oppen, ever present, for the company and the example.

Grateful acknowledgment is made to the editors and publishers of the following journals and chapbooks in which some of these poems were first published: "The Hugeness of That Which Is Missing" appeared in *Chicago Review*, thanks to Devin Johnson; it subsequently appeared as a chapbook from Shifting Units Press/Boog Literature, thanks to David Kirschenbaum. A section of "The Hugeness of That Which Is Missing" appeared, in different form, in *First Intensity*, thanks to Lee Chapman. "Line of Descent" (in an earlier form) and "Voiced Stops" appeared in *Conjunctions*, thanks to Bradford Morrow. "The Gradual All" appeared in *American Poetry Review*, thanks to Arthur Vogelsang, David Bonnano, and Stephen Berg. "Carried Across" appeared in *The Kenyon Review*, thanks to David Baker. "To C" appeared in the web journal *Slope*, thanks to Ethan Paquin. "To Virginia" appeared in *Oxford American*, thanks to Annie Wedekind. "Facing in All Directions" may or may not have appeared in *Stand* (England), thanks, in either case, to John Kinsella.

NATIONAL
ENDOWMENT
FOR THE ARTS

Manufactured in the United States of America
Book design by Sylvia Frezzolini Severance
New Directions Books are printed on acid-free paper.
First published as a New Directions Paperbook Original in 2001
Published simultaneously in Canada by Penguin Books Canada Limited

Library of Congress Cataloging-in-Publication Data

Gander, Forrest, 1956—
    Torn awake / Forrest Gander.
        p.   cm.
    ISBN 0-8112-1486-9
    I. Title
PS3557.A47T62001
811'.54—dc21   2001032657

New Directions Books are published for James Laughlin
by New Directions Publishing Corporation
80 Eighth Avenue, New York 10011

For Carolyn and Brecht,
by whom with whom in whom

This is a beautiful country. I have not cast my eyes o'er it before,
that is, in this direction.

— John Brown on his way to be hanged

And there I am
All things at once

— Hölderlin

TABLE OF CONTENTS

TORN AWAKE

FIRST

THE HUGENESS OF THAT WHICH IS MISSING

Contact

Call the direction the eye is looking
the line of sight. There
where it grazes the surface
                of the visibly surging
without reference to a field of human presence,
don't look away.
                        I haven't looked away.

The neurons spike quickly. And the catastrophe
will be consummated even to the end, to the absence of ambiguity,
a new range of feeling. Torn awake. What if
a man went into his house and leaned his hand
against the wall and the wall
                was not?

Look how your relation to truth creates a tension
you have slackened with compromise.
                        Yes, and the more
distant it is, the more I have valued it. But to stand
where the crossing happens, as fall oaks fold
                        into lake light, and so
wearing reflection, take a further step inside—

                        No, the voice said, you will strike out
into a forest of pain, unpathed, wolved, clouds muffling the mountain ridge

and spilling down in runnels,
blindness with confusion come to parle, at variance with,
measuring out an exile between self and self. Driven
transverse. Nevertheless you will begin to arrive, to know

from intimate impulse
the crucial experience of . . . the threat of dissolution of . . . but not yet.
There is something more

than rhythms of distance and presence,
of more quality than the set of qualities determining figure and ground
and suffering, where respite is so often
misinterpreted as a horizon.

Isn't the word for a turn of phrase
itself a turn of phrase?

Something was given to me as a present
and a specter was attached to me, pregnant

with equivocation.

And in the throat of language,
and in early June riots of starlings,
and in some crumbs in the seam of a book,
the solid real steps out from infinitely diluted experience
saying, *Tongue I gave you. Eyes.*

At any point in the trajectory, the body might stop. Do you recall this part?

But who is it that is speaking
in the glorious, unstrung light?

Contagion

Whose is the small voice urging,
Go ahead, jump?

           During the news, you must have fallen
                          asleep.

No, I didn't fall asleep. An electric sea was discovered
on Neptune's moon.

           That was something you dreamed.

Tar blisters from cracks in the road. As a snake arrows across,
its underscales burn and seal.

              Seconds separate sound from flash

warbling in the bellies of clouds.
How stirring and pretty before the storm wheels over
dragging its thud

        and the rain.

And now the needle lifts from the sound of grasshoppers
and friends break off like a shoelace. There is a climax of silence

                  adequate to whatever

intention I might bestow. Headlamps marrow the dark. Bats
sip nectar from moonflowers.
Each morning, the *I* from which acts go forth: picking up
a newspaper from the bed of sage, staring off
toward the neighbor's house, thoughtless.

Permission to ask anything.

Granted.

Did I piss it away in talk?   No, it knocked your breath loose.
My flesh blistered and sloughed. For what?   You would have
                                                scratched out your own eyes
                                        that you might not be distracted.
Had I stumbled toward the edge
when something happened? To hear what?   A small voice urging—
To glimpse what?   A color
                                disappears into its complement,

the day puts on evening's sleeve. Strata capture sediment
which subsides, compacts, alters. The long sleep
of diatoms crystallizing into quartz. Yet
stored in crustal rock like a magnetic tape recording
                                the memory of an originary
dynamo remains.

At any point in the trajectory, you may fold your hand.

Have you forgotten, before he crowned,   those wild breaths?
Have you forgotten   the escape of the waters?

Radiant opacity. Speaking earth. Weren't we
thick once as birds and awake together?
But something has hissed me out.

Proximity

Originary dynamo: a remanence in rock
of the paleomagnetic field. Iron grains,
aligned in magma, orient the core.
But here in the flicker between

                                  eruptions, I am
subject to an utterance with no fixed point.

The pitcher plant swallows a wren.
Each site of smooth space overlies
a tangent of Euclidean space

                            endowed with
striated dimensions, swoons, and suspenses.
She plucks from the oven a still-soggy newspaper,
glancing at the forecast: rain. Smooths her skirt

                                  behind her knees

and we leave the house together like waves
propagated in unison, in lock step. The hubcap
reflecting the wet dog's face

                           and our distorted bodies
approaching.

To say: I live on the Street of Carpenter Frogs.
To say: Goldfinch on the thistle! or,
Certain ganglion cells are excited

                         by the retinal cones.

To recognize the scent, mixed with pine-combed wind,
of mucus in one's own nostrils.

Apparent world, the book insists,
not the only one. Or is this a mistranslation?

To say: I have lost the consolation of faith
though not the ambition to worship,

to stand where the crossing happens.

Terror

Before the pulse of severe cold, in sand

beneath the arborescent heather's

                    bleak twigs,

a bluebottle fly lays its eggs in the slit of a dead starling's beak.

Who is inaccessible to fear? Startle reflex:

                         that revulsion

prior to the moment of being, a spasm

before self comes to life and fills in

the interval with a perception called pain, charging

                              the body with nausea.

A civil war in my face? Is this hunger unlike that of others?

I look up toward the earth's gleaming, silverdark rim:

the lour of cumulus, relinquished

kindness, dusk's faltering measure. And down.

Was it insignificant before I bent

my gorgeous attention over it?

Enflamed

Weeks after the service, they open a letter.

Would you please write what you knew of him, and if he ever spoke of me?

The signal of an effort, the feeling of *and* and *but*. If a deer
eats even one infected blade, its mouth and intestines ulcerate and slough.
The watch wanes, but the world keepeth, a dance of particles

                                       furling back on themselves.
A hurtling cone of blue Cherenkov light.

What holds more than it can hold?

                               Inconsolation. Astonishment,
the anti-styptic. Tongues worm back
from dry lips. The desert glows
with phosphorescent mushrooms. Specks of plutonium
from Pahute Mesa's Test Site
seep into groundwater while hours

                       gather into the authority
toward which the couple proceeds.

Incomprehensible the shouting.
She stares transfixed by his mouth
disgorging the script that wounds her. Without cruelty,
there is no circus. Sap beads at the orchid's petals. Below the mesa,
minareted cliffs. Despite avowed discontinuities, cottonwoods

                                that fringe an ephemeral river,

their sense of the world lies in the world, in the cat-urine

smell of sage. The strategy called Placing at a Distance, the doubt

subordinating the fragment "I believe in": do they cultivate these and flock

into event

only to blur the enchantment?

To ask what it means. Reign of loss. Absence like winter. To find themselves

at the aporetic center, unable to respond, blankening.

But you, in the shimmer, almost vaporous,

are you—*the small voice*—beyond

touch? Your fingers—

has sensation

overcome them? Are they past contact, to be kindled. Or

LOVE'S LETTER

TO C

Inside, inside the return, inside, the hero diminishes.

Over her vessel they place a veil, and when it is lifted

the name of the vessel has been lost. Consider

the darkness of the water which has no scent

and neither can it swallow. Yet the ship's bow

extends over the proscenium like a horse

at a fence and the orchestra stands and files out.

On the long walk home, I long to see your face.

SECOND

VOICED STOPS

Summer's sweet theatrum! The boy lunges through
The kitchen without comment, slams the door. An
Elaborate evening drama, I lug his forlorn weight
From floor to bed. Beatific lips and gap-

Toothed. Who stayed late to mope and swim, then
Breach chimneys of lake like a hooked gar
Pressing his wet totality against me. Iridescent
Laughter and depraved. Chromatic his constant state. At

Ten, childhood took off like a scorched dog. Turned
His head to see my hand wave from a window, and I too saw
The hand untouching, distant from. What fathering-
Fear slaked the impulse to embrace him? Duration:

An indefinite continuation of life. *I whirled out wings.* Going
Toward. And Lord Child claimed now, climbing loose.

Blue-pajama-tendered wrists and hands. In rest, his musical
Neck, pillowed cheek. Else by damp relentment, swal-
Lowed almost in coverlet, fetched longwise
From lashing hours into this unlikely angle, wedge,

Elbow of unfollow. Before, the nightly footfall
—*shtoom*—his bed to our bed. Scaled eyes.
(Cezanne died watching the door through which
His son did not arrive.) (Ajar, widening . . .)

Gone again to non-meridian dreams and
Murmuring broken noise in tens. To wit:
Lying bare, the sheets a husk shed low
Over the sorrel-vine of him. Midnight

Extracts me from sleep to bear witness to that one, there:
Local, small, breathing evenly, pathetic, soothe and bloom.

Nidor of match-torched tick rising from the sink, he
Hams and dishes across a heel-dinged softwood floor.
Improvised jujitsu, mind-mirrored, eyes runny, nostrils
Gleeting. His sock-feet trail dog hair and M & M's. Or

Shouts into the house: *Come out!* to see him,
A sthenic daimon, zap the driveway
With a curtain rod, the whooping
Center of a ring of spark. His last rite:

Peers into, scrupulously, both closets, under
His bed, luring the dog with milkbones. He worms
Into sheets after her, contorted to fit. *Goodnight
Mom,* etc. I sit at the edge in an intimacy without like,

And we talk in soft hues of curved space or newts
Whose bodies freeze and revive every spring.

From outside, a child's cry, blank of indecipherable
Sound, pure distress or joy to which the now
Acutely attentive body, body become
Prayer, closes every

Other tuning down.
Planted in my chair within the transparent
Room like an oak, squirrels whirling around.
But the cry does not repeat. And the boy

Should be at school. The halt-stitch
Slowly uncomes until breath begins
To assume its first position. Looming
Close, a cardinal's liquid *cue, cue,* dry

Plash of cars. Barely less green, the face
Of the ongoing in the window again.

Her whimper pitched high, the greyhound dream-
Races on kitchen tile. He scrapes back a chair
And hunches against morning's cool:
Nates to heels, knees to chin, t-shirt

Stretched over the foreshortened
Bulge of him. Bowl-of-Chex mouthfuls
Mostly open. A newspaper turns: voluptuous
Acoustics of home as bird hits

Window, walls tremble. The concussion
(Crushed breast) blots the pane (broken
Neck) with an impact mark: a solid
Host-white print the breadth

Of a child's fist from which
The ghost-trace of wingbones upcurve.

No whit poised, but given pause
At the door of his room, I quicken into
Mescalinate ecstasy, softly
Unclocked, stood irrelevant, eldering,

A guardian eloquence
Among the dank smell of him
Fecund in sleep, scratching scabs
On his throat. Loss is what

Distracts. And chiggers underpin
The mutable earth whose attributes will
Concur with those of time
While mine at cross-purposes

Careen. So
Manage my affections. Killed the light.

Constant singing, the inward rendering pungent
Undersong and wordless high lullaby wafted over a table
Of quadratic equations. Whose whirligig beetles are these
Let loose in the toilet bowl? No shut-up is there,

No sleeping late. The insistence (full gaze) of his face,
High-cheeked, his roweled pupils, peening rum-brown
Eyes, floodgates to the wonderworld, blink wide. Close.
Vertigo of veering to kiss his full lips in the blind

Room. Answerable (the gate swings out) to his summons, this
Opening in being, vast of trouble, inward savor, reprise,
Privilege of. Is gravity. Not situation. Seeing of. What is
Taking place. The yellow pine siskin chirping *to-thee, to-thee*—

To devote all wakefulness, apprise and spring
As star moss rises and purple melic.

LOVE'S LETTER

TO THE READER

Although you were looking for something else

in the mirror, you can't avoid them can you?

The wrinkles of sarcasm, the crow's-feet of insomnia,

and the bleary-eye of hesitation,

and the silent voice saying look what time it is, and your name, and why

    don't you lie down

so you'll be rested for work tomorrow.

Then the dream snaps on.

And yet a distant hope keeps you standing on your feet. You are still

standing, aren't you? Although it is late now and the question you were

    asking,

Who am I, has become something different.

What is there?

How has the tactual amnion of habit failed

to protect you? Gone from yourself, you are not alone. Although when

    you are gone,

you are not. And night discharges

itself into hills, into the river's fan gravel and swallow holes, mangrove

roots thickening around lost fish hooks. In the gas station

sign, Pegasus lights up and flickers out and lights up again

and muscles twitch in the attendant's jaw as he stares into the bay,

a timing chain part number on the slip of paper in his hand.

While stars flare and the waitress crumbs

the tablecloth, are you just opening again

to the lust to be filled with something? What is it? Around you, the nameless, countless things hullabalooing in silence

sop up your looking at the very moment of contact, at the critical

instant when your line of sight, lifted from the mirror and gently set down

again

into a groove of the revolving earth, catches

and appearance pours out like frog song.

It was me, yes, following when you led and when you fell behind.

How long it took us to get here, we who

belong to this time in all its thin passages and in

its fullness. Only let me press my mouth to the back of your hand

before you move it from my face.

THIRD

THE GRADUAL ALL

Then comes the effervescence to your eye. Arms crossed, mouth
open, tongue tip probing

                slightly bucked front teeth. When I came to it,
it was bored, biting the cuticle of its thumb and looking down
at its shoes. Perfect, I thought,

                        aroused.

—*mm*—

Then, as something bored looking down at its shoes,
cascades of myself telescoped through one another. Beyond
the limits of consecutive clauses, startled,

                            pushed you
deep into a corner. Held the haunches. Made you carry yourself
higher but without becoming short in the neck. For
you seemed to want to get it short.

—*mm*—

Then a flock of wild preparatory strokes,

                                  ecstasy of the sugar

cube crunch. Could see lineated jaw muscles

twitch in sequence. One needs,

if one is to proceed, a tense. When the movement is big

                                        and expressive.

As soon as the neck

parallels the rail. Cannot, I cannot step back,

I told you, wiping my eyes between your breasts.

                                         Give it some spur.

—————

Then, giving it some spur, I caught the rumbling

                                         and you

caught the falling down. Swerving, the sun,

utterly lightless, swerved. A slab of snow

                                seemed to lift

from the ground, turning slowly

in memory's protected space before it

rushed at your face.

                         With a muffled plush.

—————

                                        Then coconut rice

flavored with cloves and screwpine leaves, sour
lemon-grass broth, shredded cucumber, an improvised lie.
Afterward, at the hospital, I visited you,

                                full of false cheer

like a poinsettia. Ask me anything, I demanded, immortal I felt,
as a three-legged toad. You said
it is awkward to question a nude man with an axe

                                        fleeing to the right.

                        ⁓⁓⁓

Then, as a nude man with an axe fleeing to the right, I began
to excavate a parenthesis in my legible life,
a passage over-read by others. From shale

                        above coal seams, I chiseled

exquisite pyrite suns. Struck it rich,

                        posing for a photo

beside the tree trunk scarred
into an elephant lip. Couldn't have
done it without you I winked as I shut the door,
a dot of another color

                        roving behind your closed eyes.

                        ⁓⁓⁓

Then the most boresome stretch of road
I know: my own arms, neck, face,
psoriatic eyes. *Lumpenfowl,* he gestured toward the pigeons, and I
caught myself in the glass. Cutting lemon twists
for my martini with a zester. Strolling

                                through the museum,
came to a translation of the broken pottery's script:
"I put quartan fever on her to the death."

                                       Flowerless,
falling, between thumb and thumb, a man without vision, eaten

                                           out and more
strange. Nib in the air, ink
smell. Hair sewn into the comb.

                      —⁓—

Then telling your childhood story: you became

                            popular at camp
teaching them to burp the alphabet. They called you
Miss Burp. Not the left
lead. Right lead, counter canter. I asked you
for the shoulder in. Asked for the circle. I tried
to imagine the first transition
beyond which the whole rodeo unfolds.

                      —⁓—

Then, as the rodeo unfolds, a match

                                scratched

against a calculus. All but two
strips of phone numbers ripped
from the *Feeling Suicidal?* leaflet

                          you posted that morning.
It's not so bad going under the knife, I overheard. It's
coming back out. Your consciousness was dreamy.

Then went, triggering different brain cells, up

                        the skidder-road. On whose
leg had I turned to urinate but the leading authority
on hunter seat equitation. Between blue

                    snowball hydrangeas flew
smack into the window. Never try this, I told you, disturbing
my position in the saddle. And don't keep your right leg so far back.

Then, your right leg so far back, we hiked Shake Rag
Lane. The presence in your odd-numbered sentences
of the breathing particle. How to bruit your wares, you wondered,
among the thick herds of strangers I was.

                              You said we never
see a blue jay on Friday, on Friday they carry a grain of sand
to hell, help the devil bank his fires.

Then actinomycosis, also known as lumpy jaw, big jaw,
wooden tongue. Weeds mowed into a mat beside the road,

                                        and a tendril
of escaped sweet pea. Not lust but passivity
toward the desire of others, I explained. Embarrassing you.
        Again. Like the softening of a stem vowel

                              in a stressed syllable.

Then, like the softening of a stem, was every entry given

a place. An office. An orifice. As when the bird affects

a terror molt. I cannot explain those octaves

nor how they came

out of me. Migrating downstream,

the scour hole. Those who claim to hear

a blue jay on Friday hear birds that mimic

jays: mockingbirds mostly, and starlings (you said).

—*mm*—

Then nothing others did could touch me anymore. The top of my head

taken off

to reveal a terrible honking.

Excuse me—

unspoken while I escaped the place of suffering. Trying to pass it off

as a hairball. Leaving incredulity to support you

with its crushed hand. Where your back and buttocks

make an avian gesture.

—*mm*—

Then, where your back and buttocks make an avian gesture,
I planted paper-white narcissi and while I slept
something crawled into my mouth and died. I

                                 who can hear you
reading to yourself in the next room,
which is not true. Which is torture. Not able to brush your eyelashes
from my narrowed view. Was I always the only customer?
What will you have, sir? Me what myself what afflicts me most me.
The hooves jackhammer against stalls as I pass. Not one
will approach me.

—ɯɯ—

LOVE'S LETTER

TO EURYDICE

Like a man who watches from close, like a man
who watches from close the motion of a chorus, the slow
choreography back and forth, hypnotized, like that
man who goes home to drink his black water: I am.
As far as my perceptions refer to what we called
the real world, they are not certain. As far as they are certain
they do not refer to what we called real.

I was there when you began to cheat on the high notes,
gobble lines for extra air. Even at that,
you floored me. The applause, smothering. I shivered
in a cold sweat. Smothering. And when I stepped
from the theater through the cordon of mounted police,
I saw myself upside-down in a horse's eye. Though I
was prepared, a place had yet to be prepared. I rode
the Tenryu ferry under a stand-and-wait moon.
I polished the statue with beeswax.

It's beginning to have a familiar ring, isn't it?
I've instructed myself to speak more slowly. As though
I were in a play.

I stepped from the theater. I kneeled,
kneeled before the statue. *The story has a skip in it.*
What is your distance but my impatience? Lichens live
under crusts of rock for a thousand years. I will never

condescend to be a mere object of turbulent

and decisive verbs. Is leaving whom? Has left whom?

It is not Orpheus speaking. Do you even know

who is speaking? Dear Eurydice. There was a rip in your stocking.

When the cry flashed across the hills *(not your cry,*

but my own), no baffle could muffle it, every hiding place

clenched shut, and a spasm rolled out from me and over the field.

The given is given. How the past waxes fat! Overhead

is now below. There was a rip

in something. Here. No, here on this page.

Whose fingerprints are not smeared across the telling? That

third person beside you. That was my character. Il terzo incomodo.

I have instructed myself to speak more slowly. It is morning.

The fog draws back its thin lavender scent.

When I kicked off my shoes to carry you—*how could I guess*

it was the beginning of my concentration, a test—into

the cramped bedroom, a cross-marked spider crawled my foot.

Upon this intentionality another would impinge. But I

was soaked in pleasure's spittle and you

submitted your willing throat. Wailful. You were. You are.

It was later, later you met Orpheus. His wealth, his fame.

His girlish smile. He went to absurd lengths, he lied

solely to appear mysterious. He played you—

that dreary chorus wending back and forth behind him—

ridiculous *morna* songs for which we hooted him offstage,
but you swallowed it.

When the cry wrung itself from between my teeth. *What*
was the last word? Offstage? There is a sound caught
in my ears, a particular sound like the sound of a breath.
How did it go, the telling? Your face
stayed in the dirt as though you saw into it.

When the cry ricocheted from the hills and screwed
back into me, wasn't it my wakening? It was my castration.

Who is that

other one beside her, they asked. It is not Orpheus
speaking. Orpheus, used up in the rashness of his first impulse.

What was torn away is speaking.

Like flakes struck from a stone ax. Like flakes
from a stone ax, the scales have fallen from my eyes
rendering me impervious to panic. Ploughed
and harrowed my soul is. And yet. *(The rip*
is full of voices.) I cannot stop this incessant scheming.
With what word, what gambit,
might a stubborn, remnant hope contract even further
and even further into a summons?

FOURTH

LINE OF DESCENT

Against the backdark, bright

     riband flickers of heat lightning. Nearer

hills begin to show, to come clear

     as a hard, detached

          and glimmering brim

     against light lifting there. And here, pitched over

the braided arroyo choked with debris,

     a tent, its wan, cakey,

     road-rut color. On the front stake, two

green dragonflies, riding each other, pause.

     Look! cries the boy, running, the father behind him

running too—

     and the canyon opening

out in front of them its magisterial consequence, cramming

vertiginous air down its throat—

          to snatch him

     from the scarp.

Having heard the man

bellow, dikes of igneous rock

intrude a sedimentary sequence.

Squirms from his grasp. At the adjoining

campsite, a dark-haired tourist

reorients his view south

to the bordering plateau. Turns

away, a quick cut in bedding

planes. *Should they meet*

at the water pump, he imagines, stepping

onto a thin-crusted slippery clump, the flood-

odor of mule dung, and the boy

looks up at him.

When one is well-defined, is the other
uncertain? When wind-smoothed sandstone,

a torn map. The boy

and man at 6 a.m.

and the Vishnu outcrop

at fifteen hundred million years. When one
is certain. Stops the father,

heaving and empty. The sea

sloshed landward

from east to west

spilling fossils. Eyes closed,

he focuses
on a speck of pain, the speck

of *How-am-I-this-man?*

to keep it from floating away. To dig out
the dead part. Tiny red flowers

curl on long lashes beside their boots.

In and out of self-forgetfulness.

A gila woodpecker eyes them

from its hollow saguaro.

The normative allure of encounter. In

and out. Lowers

his head in voiceless spirants

as the boy, with a Swiss pocketknife,

whittles his pencil.

In Bright Angel Shale,

balled trilobites. An ant escapes

from the ant-lion and

Deus ex machina!—

the boy dangles it over

the ant-lion pit and drops it back in.

Who can peel back the observing

and climb into presence?

The man? He tries to give himself

to curiosity but is hauled back

into semblance's

desert where things of the world are

distorted. What he feels is distorted.

As though it were theater and he

were scripted no words and a terrible fear of—

And dropped, with child, into a dry,

crumbly excavation.

For want of time

                insists the father the boy

undress by the sink

                in the KOA washroom

inflexibly travertine

                a crowded assemblage of males

the boy angling in tears

                at the top of an inner gorge

for the privacy of a stall

On varved clay,

      the boy hunches at an oozing

            gap in the record. Under his boot,

                  pieces of Redwall

     break away

       and the fresh rock turns out

           to be grey. Crimson, finger-shaped

bruises

    stripe his triceps.

Fifth hour of hike: vultures jod-

jod heads from the long ramping

                boughs of a desert willow. At

this point in the father's story the boy

                    detests Odysseus

for betraying Philoctetes. Composite

                    revulsion built from

fragmentary telling.

The silts laid down. Swears,

            I will not *grip his arms*

                in anger again, the

man—

A clock we can use
to gauge term and event. A record
of transgressions. In the early
moon, the man wakes to bats—
fluttered from the same Cretaceous stock
that produced condylarths—and the boy
on his elbows *watching him.*

What is the preferred

orientation

of an early blue thrust fault? That is

grit in his mouth or is it

the immanent making

its announcement? When one is

well-defined—

The boy shears and rolls in dream

on the slippery sleeping bag

giving himself

an erection. And if each

image, each line

on the horizon yields

to another, when do the meanings of

perception dig in?

Canyon walls compress

        concordant shifts. Heat, and fossil

              footprints wink across

    the Supai. Battened to the thrill of light,

violet skinks. Clack! the boy claps

    rock with rock. A barked

        reproach evaporates

from the sedimentary progression. Slowly.

    They walk slowly

      who descend into

        beginning, like animals led

   toward an altar, the one stumbling

        under a backpack, the one dawdling to catch

    horned toads.

A caustic tongue scorching into them.

An inward face of identity

                     mimics the strata.

LOST, the stick-pierced paper says, but *what-*

                     was-lost has washed away. Come

to the edge of language, he finds the edge

is inside language. Coiled

           within him the monster

whose emotion is impatience whose tongue is hiss.

                           Aroused, the head

rises and strikes. And yet, who would not

           crawl on his belly, mouth in dust,

to know he had not ruined it? To learn

           a way out. At the stream, the boy asks

why friends would leave Philoctetes

           alone on an island. He tugs off the boy's boot,

                  massaging his chafed tendon

between thumb and forefinger.

The principle of original horizontality.
Dry heat, no sweat, empty canteens. A siesta
in late afternoon buff-light.
Fanning the sprawled boy
with a torn map
to keep off impetuous, clamoring flies.

Two hours after the major

        unconformity, the canyon's rim

eclipses the sun. Through Cambrian talus,

            pit vipers unwind — true

heirs to the pineal eye.

        A man recounts Greek plays to the boy

phosphorescent with dust

while wrens drop

        vertically through dwarf pines rooted

                in foliate schists

chirping *seed*,

            seed.

LOVE'S LETTER

TO VIRGINIA

Every new thing—the sentence began and began

to decay in the dryness of my mouth before I could finish it,

the doctor laying her ear to my chest, listening

for a dead space in the labored

breathing, her fingers probing my ribs for tenderness—

quickens me. Was it something I might insist upon as though

to convince myself?

Sometimes you are more in me than I am

in this room. Sick of myself, I know myself vaguely

as consciousness, image, thing. Here is my dimensional body.

                                      But if there is no frontier

between eloquence and world, in the realm of things

where incoherence is manifest, will we say life presents itself

to that which speaks of itself, as schist

basement rises into the Blue Ridge between valleys? Who would not

read the openness of such long-familiar eyes as a world ready

to be seen, inaugurating itself once more. And

if I received you like that?—

(now that I am vulnerable, but not against my will)

with greediness and delight, entertaining you, exhilarated where

quartz-veins sever beds of black mica in the hills and rains

etch brachiopods from Shenandoah limestone. . . . Begotten

with strange attentiveness, besotted

as I am with you, I feel my response fill in

the routine between us, gathering you into me

in shovelfuls, see myself inverted, a reflection

in a shovel's blade, alone and

desperate and miserable like something unplanted, and then

beatified, wet with intimacy, fine-

tuned to wakefulness. So to hear

tendrils rustle under dead leaves, each thing announcing

its exigence, each tendril, its godly excellence curling out

between ambiguities, to see the beetle in a laurel blossom and

ten pollen-bowed stamens, triggered,

snapping toward the center. If life presents itself. Is—

one horizon ladled into another. Near the window, fragrant

privet. Is nothing— by this means, by this meaning's benevolence,

(the inflammation promising through my lungs)—mended? What then?

FIFTH

CARRIED ACROSS

Through vidrio, a riot of birdsong. Whose face
the stranger? High cheekbones, stout chin,

                  skin pocked like cantaloupe rind.

How extensive will it be, eroding conjugation? Long
negra-azul hair rivers to the *Ahh* of her back. Glackety-
grack, the mortar wagon crossing

                        tile patio.

Black streets, one fruit stand open late: nova of color. Oh

nectarial moon, only elsewhere are you called

cliché. Lovers entwined

                             on benches.

Low whisper of night

traffic at the park's edge. What if

                                    "we" did not

                                              presuppose

national, ethnic, linguistic affiliation? What word, then, throw

at the yapping dog?

Blotting out vision, breathable air, a carbonized foulness

mushrooms

behind the bus. Her dress fades

into distance as color

blown

onto a resin sequence. Now

are grackles hooked

by the sun's aigrette, disturbed

and stern and enormous.

The unstressed fourth and invented fifth foot

of their long-voweled croaking

revives me. By the throatful.

But in this human idiom, *voices*

bleeding across frequencies, intention

torn open, the selves crowning, I experience

extended cloud. Will does not limit

what I feel. The pornography is inexhaustible.

Ruina

Casa
Para
Aves

Nido
Para
Amor

Todo
Para
Nada

                                    The cast of her torso—

        corset de yeso— upright on the bed, cleft,

the molded expression of breasts. Each

                pajaro deviates slightly from habitual song

                                and I listen *as though*

                                        to answer all.

        Vocables unloosen

        from reference. Through

                unyielding columns of cars,

                        a deaf-mute, red rag in hand, looms—

exhausted face at the windshield.

Or an ebony Christ in San Romano, head

cocked to the wall of retablos, brilliant

appeals left alone

        too long. *Encontrandose*

Eulalia Prado en condicione de perder la vista

                imploro a la virgen

                    de Rorio de Talpa

el cual da gracias por el Beneficio recibido. A lamb

      on a huge book, eagle facing upward, an eye

in a pyramid, and before each symbol on the altar box,

              a coin slot. The translation.

                    Invented their own

writing and vigesimal scale. I am — *crumbled*

dust. In 69 A.D.,

says the glyphic script, Ah Cracaw

                              took Jaguar Paw

prisoner. Plopped his children in clay vessels, a jade bead

in each mouth. Across cleavage planes

                    in his earrings, my reflection splays,

    my obsidian-

        pupiled eyes.

Fifteen ways of perforating and filing teeth

        encrusted

with gems

   carved from limestone, basalt,

pyroclastic rock. All but three

      Mayan codices

        were burned

to clear the slab for Christ. Truth

   is structured, I scribbled, like language.

Which language? Hill of grasshoppers. Altar

of skulls. Says of her own work that sincerity

   and veracity are distinct. Has no interest

       in sincerity. Ocean of cloud

lapping the volcano.

The unglazed figure reaching behind

to wipe himself. A past that never stops

        changing its expression. I am alive,

he wrote, and cannot bear

        to be unworthy of my life. Came to the end

      of words and waited. Then *things* restore silence, speaking

of themselves. Lizards

        lick shadow under the dry fountain. Lidless gaze.

The butt and very dustmark of my utmost journey.

                  Pain as utterance

    withheld.

On the white stucco wall, a cat

                                 closes its eyes

              to the clang of machetes in musical phrases

with drags from a cigarette

                    for rests. The surround is whistling,

an aggregate sound

with sweet singularities in the flamboyanes. A policeman

smoking against the gate

            of a residencia, Rotweiler

                                heaped by his boots.

                  Jacaranda, fuchsia, camellia

pink. Ornithologists know the songs of birds, who

                  knows their thoughts? Translation alone

births the untranslatable. Listen, Señor,

                                  I have been used

by my own ignorance, self-disgust, my instinct

for failure. Pray for me.

Every poem suggests it, suggests its own—

                    Coffined-in, the bus weaving

dim streets. Foredawn begins

to colonize space

around me, to colorize distance: trees greening, dawn

          parcels out sinople walls and roofs

                              go ochre before

                                        the spectral,

dusty highway. Words ripen my difference

from the world. A spasm

burrowing into my eye.

Incomparable odor from the tortilleria, yeasty-flour
sour blue-baked smoke flavors the air. Twin girls
bunch beneath the yellow and white umbrella.

                              Workman
in a hole in the road, a parasol
on its side shading him. Hindpaw bandaged,
a dog observes from the esquina
near the emptied jail.

                              Which speech
does not incarnate presence? Just a moment,
Señor, executioner.

                              The barber

sleeps in a cane chair outside his shop. Musics mix

                  along cobbled streets. In high heels,

women tracked by furtive eyes

        from the portales. Torqued grotesquely

           and biting its own rump in the park. A form

                            of meditation for me.

Like pheromone trails traced by ants, the meeting places

of glances. And every minute around the zócalo,

              expectancy of more. Picking a fresh scab

         above the hairline of my neck.

Only some red

and blue wash and the figures of a family drawing
their own blood. Two thousand years gone, a hand
paused before this lintel, thinking. The hand poised

in my mind.
The sign
announces *Basura Peatonal*, "walking rubbish." Of things
ill done and done ill toward.

Marta, Paula, Lope,
and Alima Alma raced to the top of the temple pyramid, HERE

to graffiti their names.
Swallows rake the field,
mesmerizing me. To read the script
of their flight is to conceive in parabolas. Rhythms combing out
knots of habit. Face to the wall,
the haircut costs 60 pesos. Who would not pay 80

for a haircut with landscape?

LOVE'S LETTER

TO THE INVISIBLE WORLD

At once, he rose from his seat, bared his right shoulder, set his knee
on the floor and, respectfully folding his hands, addressed them thus:

The trace on my lips of her nipples' rouge improves the taste of the wine.

*Asleep, she is completely closed, windowless, contained by the world in its dark
while also she illuminates some portion of that world, the portion
where I remain, entranced.*

Thrash-polka on her radio, a bluegill on her line.

*To what can I compare her conversation's surprise?
Karl Jansky built an antenna to study shortwave interference
but he discovered radio galaxies.*

*From the fricative heat of her limbs when she walks,
the forest blooms beside her, berries ripen.*

*Her quick cries of pleasure:
I am held awake listening for their return.*

Her eyes constitute a disorder, a methodical perplexity.

Love solves nothing, though it has made me appear.

She is a prism through which light intensifies. Her voice, a stringed paulownia.

Her great originality, her liveliness, an incessant bursting forth of identification, enthusiasm coincident with the forever ungraspable.

There was a ground swell of low murmuring. Then the head monk called,
    Next.

SIXTH

FACING IN ALL DIRECTIONS

Resting on her belly, her long-fingered hands suggest she is pregnant. It

might be

September, when the full-bore orchestration of insects rusts out, goes tinny.

By the way he has raised his hand to her face
as though it were an innovation on faces or merely the envelope
for his admiring, as though a hand could say *thou* —we recognize them,
lovers who have rushed

to the wood's edge

on trails of inference
through all the thicknesses of scattered and divergent signs,
flying the contagion. What plague this time? What time?
As if there were a safe house, some renunciation to grope toward. Look:
he is still a boy even, an eagerness

he has let her pare

into the avowal that unlocked her eyes. And if

in his pocket he carries a flute carved
from the hollow ulna of a red-crowned crane,
and if in her kiss he can taste black pills she has swallowed to stop
the bleeding, it is not in the brief conspectus of

their history according to Dürer

who shows us, *us alone*, the skeleton behind them
unleaning from a tree
as a tense might be unbound. The couple pause

to appraise each other, their miraculous escape

from a fatality

that leads precisely here. As it always does.

But warning birds have yet to fly up in their faces. Briefly,
however briefly, they outstrip ordination.

<div style="text-align:center">~~~</div>

Then the sun's limb darkens, clouds roll in, and when rains let up
no one is there. Only two stalk-eyed flies fighting on a stump. In a

distant city

once named for the white thighs of its women, pigeons
blister Sacre Couer's dome. Dim, early morning, on Blvd. St.-Germain,
phalanxes of sycamore thicken with seed balls. Raiding
the palace, a grimy throng rouses the queen from sleep.
As hallways swell with shouting, she gathers herself

into her gown

and stumbles to the ante-room
known as the *Oeil-de-Boeuf.* Although she rehearsed
these moments, each gesture is fraught, each effort invested
in others, an architecture of ornament she cannot begin to put together.
What a quivering in the walls as the great doors bow inward. Like candles
on a sumptuous table,

the evenly-spaced steps of her fleeing,

the little coils of scent swirling up from each footprint
conspire to weigh her down. And while she pounds at the king's chamber,

a single bellow

fills the hall of mirrors, as though a huge mouth were coming

to swallow the remaining ripe hours

already dished for her to try.

Always: as though a huge mouth were coming.

But days warm and the tourists walk on

through the palace, through an incessant storm of cometary grains,

                                       swayed by plans for lunch,

by rear-guard obligations. One shopping cart

rammed into another. Little failures leading to blankness.

The Seine rises and oceans rise and from their lightless floors, giant worms,

                                                mouthless

and gutless, wave.

                       —*m*—

                            Dear C, do you remember finding

this rock in the garden? Grey-blue silicious slate. It burrowed up

through the million years of sedimentary facies

between begotten

                    and born. Events

occur as discourse, it's true, but who

would read the stone or say at such-and-such a point, at these coordinates of

                                August luster

and the ratcheting of cicadas, it entered the drama

                    interrupting life as it was lived and known.

It brought no plague; it has no mouth — a word

I write and see your mouth, the star

in your lower lip where once your tooth went through.

No warning birds. No slackening of the river.

~~~

An alluvial scar incised

by a river is like the gnash of arriving through thought at words. And words

themselves can be compared to stones,

relentless systems of reference. On the island of Cyprus, amid rubble

from the earthquake that obliterated Kourion

in 365 A.D., they found

the skeletons of a young man,

a woman, and their eighteen month old child.

The man's arm circled the woman's waist, his left leg,

as though to shield her,

he had thrown across her pelvis. He held her hand and clutched the child.

Bliss comes uncounting the hour, seizing no set moment. Some

claim there isn't time to consider the whole of the story or

the interdependence of its characters. Some say every meaning will be

revealed until the last witness is lost and gone.

NOTES

For the prefatory quote by John Brown, I am grateful to Susan Howe.

In *The Hugeness of That Which Is Missing*, the title of which comes from George Oppen's *Daybooks*, "the watch wanes but the world keepeth" is a variation on a line from Ezra Pound's translation of "The Seafarer." "Without cruelty there is no circus" is adapted from Kant, "intimate impulse" from Milton. This poem is for my friend, Peter Weltner.

In *Unvoiced Stops*, "I whirled out wings" is, of course, from Gerard Manley Hopkins. The only person I've ever heard use the word "shtoom" in unaffected conversation is Peter Sacks.

"Love's Letter: To Virginia" is for Rod Smith.

"Love's Letter: To the Invisible World" is for improvisatory monk and poet, John High.

"Of things ill done and done ill toward" in the last stanza of *Carried Across* is a variation of a line from T. S. Eliot's "Little Gidding": "Of things ill done and done to others' harm/ Which once you took for exercise of virtue." Several words from Henry Vaughan's "Distraction" are incorporated into the sequence. The skinny poem in Spanish beginning "Ruina" is my transcription of a handwritten note on Frida Kahlo's desk. This poem is for Harryette Mullen who was a large and wonderful part of the adventure.

New Directions Paperbooks—A Partial Listing

For a complete listing request a free catalog from
New Directions, 80 Eighth Avenue, New York 10011   †Bilingual

For a complete listing request a free catalog from
New Directions, 80 Eighth Avenue, New York 10011

†Bilingual